Code Cracking

Story by George Ivanoff

Illustrations by Francesca Ficorilli

Contents

Chapter 1

Op Shop Treasure

"Oh, wow!" breathed Eddie. "Would you look at that!"

"What?" asked Gemma, hands on hips. "It's just a book, and it looks like it's about to fall apart."

"It's old!" said Eddie. "I love old books." He gently picked up the battered book and held it in his hands. "But it's more than that. It's a book about William Shakespeare's plays."

"Oh!" Suddenly Gemma seemed more interested.

William Shakespeare was a famous writer who wrote many well-known plays, like *Hamlet* and *Romeo and Juliet*, and lived a long time ago in England. Eddie thought it might have been in the 1600s ... or maybe the 1500s. He wasn't sure.

Eddie and Gemma were best friends. They were both eleven and in Year 6 at Mayview School. They both had brown hair, although Gemma's was cut in a bob and Eddie's was really short. They were both the same height – average. Gemma wore glasses and Eddie had braces on his teeth.

Eddie and Gemma were also both members of the Theatre Club at school. They had gone to visit their local second-hand charity shop to look for anything that might be useful for their club. It seemed like a good way to spend their Saturday morning while Eddie's dad did the weekly shopping at the supermarket. The two friends were after anything that could be used as props and costumes – toy swords, fancy dress, funny hats ... whatever!

So far, they hadn't found anything useful, so Eddie had dragged Gemma over to the book section. He loved reading and he was always searching for new books to add to his ever-growing collection. Although, in this case, it was *old* books. And the book he was now holding was very old indeed. It had a hard cover and was bound in dark-red cloth, with the title in gold lettering. The title was faded and half scratched off, but it was still readable.

ALL THE WORLD'S A STAGE

The Theatrical World of William Shakespeare

Eddie carefully started to lift the cover, but the spine almost fell off. He quickly closed it up again.

"It might fall apart if I open it," said Eddie, worry creasing his brow.

"It's a book!" said Gemma. "It's no good unless you can open it up and read it."

"Yeah, I know," said Eddie, frowning. "Maybe I'll buy it and then look at it carefully when I get home."

"How much is it?" asked Gemma.

Eddie turned the book over in his hands, but couldn't find a price. He shrugged and carefully took it up to the front counter.

The elderly lady took the book from him and examined it. Eddie winced as she turned it over and looked inside the cover. He was certain the book would fall apart if she wasn't careful, and it didn't look like she was being careful.

"That's odd," she finally said. "It doesn't seem to have a price on it, and it's not in very good condition, is it? We don't normally put books that look like they're about to fall apart out on the shelves." She huffed. "You can have it for a dollar, if you want."

Eddie nodded and handed over the money.

Chapter 2

Book Repairs

Eddie placed the ancient-looking book on his desk, then he and Gemma stared at it.

"All the World's a Stage," read Gemma. Then she finished off the famous quote, "And all the men and women merely players."

"It's from *As You Like It*, isn't it," said Eddie. "I went to see that play with my parents when it was at the local theatre."

"I missed it," said Gemma. "It was all sold out by the time my parents got around to booking." She sighed. "Anyway … are you going to open the book now?"

Eddie carefully reached out and lifted the cover. It came off in his hands and he gasped. "Oh, no!"

Eddie put the front cover on the desk next to the rest of the book. The spine had also fallen off, revealing the loose string that was meant to be holding all the pages together.

Gemma pointed to the handwritten note at the top right-hand corner of the front page.

This book belongs to E H (36).

Shall I compare this book to a summer's day?

"I wonder what that means," said Gemma.

"I think it means that someone really loved this book," said Eddie. "It's a line from one of Shakespeare's love poems, but it's been changed. Instead of 'Shall I compare *thee* to a summer's day?' it says 'Shall I compare *this book* to a summer's day?'"

"That's weird," said Gemma.

Eddie was still staring at the book. "I'm going to have to fix the book before I can read it," he said.

"Are you sure it's worth it?" asked Gemma. "You could just read it like it is."

"But then it would fall apart," said Eddie.

"So what?" asked Gemma with a shrug. "Then after you've read it, you can throw it out. I mean, it only cost one dollar."

"It's not the money," said Eddie as he examined the book carefully. "There's something about this book. It ..." He hesitated. "It's special." He pointed at the writing. "It meant a lot to someone, so ... I want to take care of it."

"Uh … okay," said Gemma. "So how are you going to fix it? Sticky tape?"

"No, I'm going to fix it properly."

"Do you know anything about fixing books?" asked Gemma.

"No, not really," admitted Eddie. "But I'm sure the internet will be able to help me out."

Eddie turned on his laptop and began searching. It didn't take long for Gemma to lose interest and head home.

Eventually, Eddie found some clear instructions on repairing hardcover books and spent the rest of the day carefully putting the book back together – tightening the strings, gluing the spine, reattaching the cover with fabric tape he borrowed from his mum.

When he finished, he put the book aside, determined not to look at it until the next day. He needed to give the glue time to dry properly. He didn't want the book falling apart again after all the work he had put into it.

The next morning was Sunday, and Eddie woke bright and early, the chirping birds outside his window pulling him out of his slumber. He rubbed his bleary eyes and looked over at the clock on his bedside table.

7:15 am.

What? Eddie groaned, annoyed that the birds had woken him so early, and shut his eyes again. He wondered if he'd be able to get back to sleep. Then he remembered the book and a sudden thrill of excitement coursed through him. Had his repairs worked? Would he finally be able to read the book without it falling apart?

He jumped out of bed and rushed over to his desk. He stared at the book, almost too scared to pick it up. With a deep breath, he reached out his hand and lifted the cover. It was a bit stiff … but it opened … and the book didn't fall apart.

Eddie took the book over to his bed and flipped through the pages, stopping when he noticed some scribbled writing in the margins. Scrawled lettering in pencil filled the margins on both sides of the page. There was even some writing in the white space between paragraphs.

But it didn't make any sense.

Letters were grouped into what should have been words, but the words weren't really words. The not-words were grouped into sentences, but the sentences made no sense either. He tried to read the first sentence.

Ymj bfw mfx gjlzs.

What did it mean?

7:15

He continued to flick through the pages of the book and noticed that notes had been scribbled on many of them. None of them made sense – no sense at all.

Why would anyone do this? he wondered.

The idea of writing in the pages of a book like this filled Eddie with horror. He loved reading and he loved books, so he took great care of all the books he owned. He never bent the covers or folded the corners of pages, and he never *ever* wrote in them.

Writing in a book was already bad, but writing nonsense in a book was even worse!

Chapter 3

What's in a Name?

"Look at this!" Eddie handed the book to Gemma.

"Oh, great!" she said, turning the book over in her hands, examining it. "You fixed it. It's not falling apart any more."

"No, that's not what I mean," said Eddie. "Look inside the book."

Gemma opened the book to a random page, frowning down at it. Then she looked at Eddie and shrugged.

"Keep looking through the pages," said Eddie. "There's writing in there."

Gemma snorted. "It's a book! Of course there's writing in it."

"No," snapped Eddie. "Handwriting! Someone scribbled notes on some of the pages."

"So what?" asked Gemma. "Lots of people make notes in their books, especially if they're school books." She smiled at her friend. "Not everyone is as overprotective of their books as you."

Eddie sighed. "That's not what I mean. Find one of the pages, look at the actual words that have been scribbled there and try to read them."

Gemma flipped through the pages until she came to one with scrawled notes. "Oh," she said, looking down at the scrabbled writing. "I see what you mean."

"What do you think it is?" asked Eddie.

"Could be some sort of coded message," suggested Gemma.

"A coded message!" Eddie's eyes lit up with barely contained excitement.

"Yeah," said Gemma, as she squinted at the writing. "It looks like words in a sentence. It's just that the words don't mean anything." She pointed to one of the sentences. "But look at the way you have short words and long words, just like in an ordinary sentence."

Gemma looked up at Eddie. "Yep. I reckon it's code, all right!"

Eddie took the book back and gazed at the meaningless words. He wanted to know what they said. Maybe it was a message from the original owner of the book.

"So … all we have to do is crack the code." There was excitement in Eddie's voice. "I used the internet to fix the book. Maybe I could use the internet to crack the code."

"Maybe," agreed Gemma.

Eddie raced over to his laptop and turned it on. He quickly typed "secret codes" into the search field, but his face fell when he saw the results. There were over three million pages.

"So many," he whispered. "This could take ages."

"Maybe," said Gemma again.

"Why do you keep saying that?" asked Eddie. As he looked over at his friend, he saw that she was holding the book again, staring at the first page. "What are you looking at?" he asked.

"The note on the first page," replied Gemma. "It's not in code. It says 'This book belongs to E H (36). Shall I compare this book to a summer's day?'"

"So?" said Eddie.

"So …" replied Gemma, "it might be a clue."

Eddie took the book back and read: "'This book belongs to E H.' And then there's a number in brackets." He looked at Gemma again. "You think the number might be the clue?"

"Maybe."

"It might be a page number?" Eddie excitedly turned the pages.

Page 36 was the start of a new chapter. The chapter was called "King Lear", which was also the title of one of Shakespeare's famous plays. There were no scribbled notes on this page. No clue.

Eddie sighed his disappointment. He was about to close the book again, when he noticed a circled word. No ... not just a word. It was a name.

Eddie's eyes widened as he realised that it wasn't just any name. It was his name!

He held the book out so that Gemma could see. Below the chapter title was a list of characters that were in the play. The name "Edmund" had been circled.

"So the E H who owned this book," said Gemma, "his first name was Edmund. Same as you."

Eddie never used the name Edmund because he didn't like it. He thought it sounded too old-fashioned. Too stuffy. Too unfriendly. That's why he called himself Eddie, which he thought sounded much nicer. No one called him Edmund, except his mum when she was frustrated with him.

He was amazed that the previous owner of this book shared his name. Eddie wondered what this Edmund thought of his name. Then he pushed these thoughts aside as he remembered there was more important stuff to think about: the code!

"This doesn't help us decode the writing," said Eddie.

"It might," said Gemma. "We now know that the content of the book is important. It's given us the owner's name, so maybe it can give us a clue to decoding the writing."

Chapter 4
The Caesar Shift

Gemma flipped through the book until she came to the page where the scribbled notes began. It was the first page of Chapter 5, which was about the play *Julius Caesar.*

"Edmund has underlined the name 'Caesar' in the chapter title," said Gemma. She ran her finger along the text and read the last line of text on the page out loud. "Public opinion in Rome then shifted against Brutus." She paused. "'Shifted' is underlined. Well, actually, just the first part of the word … 'shift'."

"Caesar," said Eddie. "And shift. What's that supposed to mean?"

"No idea," admitted Gemma. "But I reckon it must be some kind of clue."

"I guess we could try another search," said Eddie, turning back to his computer.

He typed the words "Caesar", "shift" and "code" into the search engine, and with a deep breath hit "enter". The first result was titled "Caesar Shift Cipher".

"What does 'cipher' mean?" asked Eddie.

"Hang on," said Gemma, as she whipped out her

phone and entered "cipher" into the dictionary app. "It's a type of code in which individual letters are changed."

"Oh," said Eddie. He grinned. "Well, that was easy, then!"

Eddie clicked on the link. Gemma leaned over him and together they read about the Caesar Shift Cipher.

Julius Caesar was a military leader in ancient Rome. When sending messages to his generals, Caesar would send them in code. He would shift the letters by three to the left, so that the letter A would become D, the letter B would become E, and so on.

There was a table to show how it worked. To encode a message, you found each letter in the top row and changed it to the one in the bottom row. To decode a message, you did the opposite.

A	B	C	D	E	F	G	H	I	J	K	L	M
D	E	F	G	H	I	J	K	L	M	N	O	P
N	O	P	Q	R	S	T	U	V	W	X	Y	Z
Q	R	S	T	U	V	W	X	Y	Z	A	B	C

"We've cracked the code!" cried Eddie. "Gemma, read out the letters of the first word and I'll decode it."

"Here goes," said Gemma. "YMJ."

Eddie decoded each of the letters and wrote them down in his notebook.

"Oh, no," he said. His voice was full of disappointment. "It didn't work."

He held up the notebook to show Gemma. It read "VJG".

"So it's not Caesar's code," whined Eddie. "Now what do we do?"

"Go back to the website," suggested Gemma. "See if it says anything else about the code."

"There," said Eddie, skimming over the information. "You can shift the letters any number of places. It doesn't have to be three, like Caesar did." He looked at Gemma. "But how many places did Edmund shift?"

Gemma looked at the page in the book and smiled.

"How about trying five?" she said. "After all, we're at the start of Chapter 5."

"Good idea," agreed Eddie.

He drew a table in his notebook just like the one on the screen. Instead of three spaces, he moved the letters five spaces so the letter A became F, the letter B became G, and so on.

A	B	C	D	E	F	G	H	I	J	K	L	M
F	G	H	I	J	K	L	M	N	O	P	Q	R

N	O	P	Q	R	S	T	U	V	W	X	Y	Z
S	T	U	V	W	X	Y	Z	A	B	C	D	E

"Okay," Eddie finally said. "Let's try it again."

Gemma read out the letters of the first word again, as Eddie decoded each letter.

"Success!" he shouted. "We have our first word. It's 'the'!"

"Well, that's not very exciting," said Gemma. "How about we finish the sentence?"

Again, Gemma read out the letters for each word and, again, Eddie decoded them. When he had finished, he looked up at Gemma with a grave expression. Slowly he lifted up the notebook so she could read it.

The war has begun.

Chapter 5

Camp

Eddie and Gemma finished decoding the writing on the first page. It made Eddie feel strange, because the words sounded like they had been written by a frightened kid.

> *The war has begun. I am scared. I do not know what will happen to my family and me. This is not our country. We are new here. People don't like me.*

"It's like a diary entry," said Gemma. "It feels weird reading someone else's diary without their permission."

"Maybe we should try to return it to Edmund," suggested Eddie.

"How do we do that?" asked Gemma.

"Clues!" said Eddie. "Edmund left clues for what his name was and he left clues for the code. Maybe there are also clues for finding him."

"I guess," agreed Gemma.

The two friends spent most of Sunday morning working on deciphering the scrawled writing. They discovered that Edmund was German and that he and his family had emigrated to Australia. They had left Germany to escape something, but it didn't say what.

In Australia, they faced discrimination. When war came, people here didn't like German people. Or Italian people. Or Japanese people. It made Edmund sad. He and his family were taken away and put in a camp with lots of other people. It was not a happy place. It felt like a prison.

A lot of the diary entries were about Edmund not understanding what was happening.

Finally, they came to a page with just one sentence:

I am an enemy alien.

"What does that mean?" asked Gemma.

Eddie shrugged silently. It made him think of science fiction stories and aliens from another planet invading Earth. Enemy aliens! But those were just make-believe. What had happened to Edmund seemed very real.

"Let's try another page," suggested Eddie.

Gemma flipped through some pages before she found another entry. Somehow it looked different, but she couldn't work out why. It was just a feeling. She began to read out the letters so that Eddie could decode them.

"Stop!" called Eddie, after three words. "It's not working."

Gemma looked at the notebook and sighed. The three words were just jumbles of letters that made no sense.

"He must have changed codes," said Eddie. "We'll have to figure out what the new one is."

"I'm tired," said Gemma. "I think I've had enough for today. And I've still got homework to do before school tomorrow."

After Gemma went home, Eddie tried to crack the code himself. He looked up random codes on the internet, but none of them worked. He looked for clues on the page that the new coded messages started on. It was a page about the play *Hamlet*. At first he missed the clue, but then Eddie noticed a faintly underlined word in a quote from the play.

I most powerfully and potently believe,
yet I hold it not honesty
to have it thus set down,
for yourself, sir,
shall grow old as I am,
if like a crab you could go backward.

The word "backward" was underlined. Eddie quickly typed "backward code" into the search engine and … bingo! Results appeared for the Backwards Alphabet Code. It worked in a similar way to the Caesar Shift. You had a list of all the letters, and lined it up with another list in backwards order.

A	B	C	D	E	F	G	H	I	J	K	L	M
Z	Y	X	W	V	U	T	S	R	Q	P	O	N

N	O	P	Q	R	S	T	U	V	W	X	Y	Z
M	L	K	J	I	H	G	F	E	D	C	B	A

He quickly tried it out, but it didn't work.

That was it. Eddie had had enough for the moment. Feeling hungry, he realised that he'd completely forgotten about lunch. So he went to get himself a snack to keep him going until dinner. Then he thought it would be a good idea to finish his homework.

That night, he had trouble falling asleep because he kept thinking about Edmund. Eddie had to find out who Edmund was, and he had to decode the rest of the diary. Eddie needed to know what had happened to this mysterious boy from the past who shared his name.

Maybe tomorrow he would ask for help.

Chapter 6

History Lesson

Mr Sanderson studied the notebook Eddie had given him. "You say that this is someone's diary?" he asked.

Eddie nodded.

"And that it was written in the margins of a book about Shakespeare?" continued Mr Sanderson.

"That's right," said Gemma.

"Fascinating." Mr Sanderson finished reading the decoded entries and looked up at the students. Mr Sanderson ran the school's history club every Tuesday lunchtime, so Eddie thought it would be a good idea to ask him about what Edmund had written.

"During the two world wars," he said, "German people weren't trusted here. Back then, Germany was the enemy, so if someone had a German background, people thought they might be a spy. It didn't matter how long they had been living in Australia."

Mr Sanderson held up the notebook. "I'd say this was from World War Two because it mentions Japanese and Italian people. Japan wasn't involved in World War One and Italy was on our side in that war. But in World War Two, Germany, Italy and Japan were all enemy countries."

"It seems silly," said Eddie.

"Well," said Mr Sanderson, "war isn't usually sensible. People suffer, and it isn't only the soldiers. Anyway, during World War Two, German-born people were classified as 'enemy aliens'. They had to be registered and they weren't allowed to travel without permission. Eventually the Australian government set up internment camps, and German-born people were put into them. It was to keep them all together, away from everyone else, so they couldn't do any spying. It was a bit like being put into prison, really. In fact, some old prisons were used as internment camps. Sometimes these camps also held prisoners of war who had been captured."

"That's really sad," said Eddie.

"And unfair," added Gemma.

Mr Sanderson sighed. "It *was* a very unfair thing to do, but people were scared. And fear often makes people do unfair things." He handed the notebook back to Eddie. "So, is that what you wanted to know?"

"I think so," said Eddie.

"Thanks, Mr Sanderson," said Gemma.

Chapter 7

Old Books

"Are you sure this is a shop?" asked Gemma. "Is it even open?"

Eddie pointed to a faded and cracked sign above the wooden door. Gemma could just make out the words "OLD BOOKS".

"I come here to browse books, sometimes," explained Eddie. "I never buy anything, because they're all really expensive, but I like looking at them."

"Doesn't the owner get annoyed at that?" asked Gemma.

"Nah," responded Eddie. "Mum and Dad know her. She's the daughter of a friend of theirs."

The door was down a little lane on the edge of the shopping village. But there weren't any other shops in this lane … just this one door. Eddie had dragged Gemma there on the way home from school today.

He pushed open the door and a little bell tinkled. As they entered, they were hit by the smell of old books – a funny kind of smell, dusty and musty, but comforting. Eddie liked it and he breathed in deeply, filling his lungs.

The shop was small and dim, with large bookshelves stretching up to the high ceiling. Each one of them was crammed full of books, and even more books sat in stacks on the floor. To one side was a locked glass cabinet with really old ones that was labelled "Antiquarian books". Gemma noticed the prices and gulped. There was nothing under $500 in that cabinet.

Eddie led the way between two of the shelves, to the other side of the room.

There was a large old-fashioned desk in the corner which was, of course, covered in books piled up high. A head popped up from behind the books. An explosion of ginger curls and a smiling face crammed with freckles greeted them.

"Hey there, Eddie-boy," said the woman. "Have you come to not buy books again?" She laughed.

"Yeah, sort of," said Eddie.

"Who's your friend?"

"This is Gemma."

"Well, hey there, Gemma-girl, friend of Eddie-boy. I'm Rosie-Rose. What can I not sell you today?"

"Actually, Rosie," said Eddie, "I've got a book to show you."

"Well, colour me interested," said Rosie, as she shifted some book stacks and made space on the desk. "Let's see!"

Eddie fished *All the World's a Stage* from his schoolbag and handed it over.

Rosie held the book, carefully turning it over in her hands, examining its surface. She slowly lifted it up to her face and closed her eyes, then took in a deep breath. She sighed as she opened her eyes again. Then, unexpectedly, her tongue darted out to taste the spine.

Gemma winced, glancing sideways at Eddie.

"Hmmm." Rosie placed the book on the desk, gently opened the cover, and began turning the pages.

Gemma watched curiously. This strange woman seemed to have forgotten that Gemma and Eddie were there. All her attention was focused on the book as she continued to turn its pages. Was she going to go through the whole book like this? wondered Gemma.

She was about to interrupt, but Eddie placed a hand on her arm. "Just wait," he whispered.

So they waited and watched as Rosie went through every page of the book. When she was finished, she looked up at them and lifted an eyebrow.

"Well, this book is quite a find, Eddie-boy," she said. "It's not in brilliant condition but it's still worth a fair bit of money. It looks like it's been repaired recently. Enough to make it readable, but not a very professional job. I reckon it's just a matter of time before it falls apart, which, of course, lowers the value."

Now it was Eddie's turn to wince. He'd been so proud of the repair job.

"The imprint page is missing," Rosie went on, "so I can't give you the exact year of publication. But based on the paper and the cover, I'd say it was early twentieth century ... somewhere around the 1930s, give or take. Quite a number of pages have notes scribbled on them and they appear to be in code. That, of course, lowers the value of the book again. If the notes had been made by someone famous, that might've increased the value, but, sadly, they weren't." She paused and closed her eyes, as if deep in thought. "I'd be prepared to offer you seventy-five dollars." She opened her eyes and looked at Eddie.

"I don't want to sell it," said Eddie. "I want to find out who the owner is."

"That'd be someone named Edmund Hagen," said Rosie.

Eddie's mouth dropped open. "How do you know that?"

"We worked out the first name because it was circled on page 36," said Gemma, "but how could you know his last name?"

Rosie smiled. "There's one letter underlined on each of the next five pages. That's pages 37 to 41. Put them together and they spell 'Hagen'."

"Wow!" whispered Gemma.

"What about the coded writing?" asked Eddie eagerly, hoping she might be able to solve the deciphering problem for them.

"The first one looks like a Caesar Shift." Rosie opened the book to where the notes started. "Okay, Chapter 5, so I'd try shifting the letters by five."

"Double wow!" said Gemma.

"That's what we did," said Eddie.

"But things change here," said Rosie, flipping through the pages. "It's all been in pencil up until now, but here the writer is using a ballpoint pen. The word 'backward' is underlined, so it's going to be either the Backwards Alphabet Code or maybe the Reverse Letter Code."

"I tried the Backwards Alphabet one and it didn't work," said Eddie.

"Hmmm." Rosie studied the handwriting with a frown, then her face brightened. "Okay … this three-letter word, 'JMY', appears a few times. That word is most likely 'the'. If we reverse the letters, it's 'YMJ', which still doesn't make sense. But if you then apply the Caesar Shift, it becomes 'the'." She smiled. "So … you need to reverse the letters in each of the words, then apply the Caesar Shift."

"Cool!" said Gemma.

Rosie flipped through some more pages. "Now, here things change again. This is the last note. It's quite short, and it's been written in felt-tip pen. And the code has also changed."

"What is it this time?" asked Gemma.

"This one is tricky." Rosie frowned. "See how there are numbers in among the letters?"

The two friends nodded.

"There are also a few symbols. See?" she said, running her finger along the text, pointing to a "+" and a "$". "I think this is a custom code."

"What does that mean?" asked Eddie.

"It means that someone has created their own code. Rather than following a pattern, they have replaced letters with random letters, numbers and symbols. This sort of code is much harder to crack. You really need to have the key in order to decode it."

"Oh." Eddie's face fell.

The bell over the door tinkled and a customer walked in. As Rosie went off to serve the customer, Eddie fished his notebook and pen from his bag. Then he and Gemma got to work on decoding the second lot of notes, the ones that used the Reverse Letter and Caesar Shift codes.

It's been a long time since I've written anything in here. I had forgotten all about this book. I am probably too old to be playing with codes now. Is fifteen too old to play? My father thinks so. He thinks I need to spend more time studying. He keeps saying that education is the key to opportunity, and he wants me to have the opportunities he didn't have. I don't want to let him down. I know how hard life has been for him and my mother.

But I like codes and I like the fact that no one can read my thoughts unless I tell them the code.

And so it continued. It was now just an ordinary diary about teenaged life – bullies at school; a girl that he liked; how he wasn't very good at maths; that he liked studying history.

Rosie finished with her customer and returned to Eddie and Gemma.

"So how's it going?" she asked.

"You were right," said Eddie.

"But there's nothing here that tells us who this Edmund Hagen was," said Gemma.

Rosie looked at them thoughtfully. "Where did you get the book?" she asked. "Whoever you got it from might know something about this Edmund."

"We got it from an op shop," said Gemma.

"Well, why don't you go back there and ask about it?" suggested Rosie. "I know it's a long shot, but someone there might know where it came from."

Eddie and Gemma looked at each other. Why hadn't either of them thought of doing that?

"Sometimes," said Rosie, smiling, "the simplest approach is the best."

Chapter 8

Back to the Op Shop

Eddie placed the book on the counter. It was Saturday again, so he and Gemma had tagged along for his dad's weekly shopping trip. It was the only way to get to the op shop. Since it shut at three o'clock on weekdays, they couldn't visit it on the way home from school.

"I wonder if you could help us?" Eddie said to the elderly lady behind the counter. "I bought this book here last Saturday. I'm trying to track down the person it used to belong to. Is there anything you could tell us about the book?"

The lady stared at Eddie and Gemma through thick glasses, which made her eyes look huge.

"You're kidding, aren't you?" she said, her forehead creasing. "Is this your idea of a silly joke?"

"N-no," stammered Eddie.

"We really are trying to find the original owner," added Gemma.

"Oh!" The woman looked a little confused. "People just leave stuff at the back door. Most of the time, we have no idea who's making the donation."

"We know the owner's name, if that helps." Eddie hopefully opened the book and pointed to the initials. "It's Edmund Hagen."

The lady stared at the initials. "I beg your pardon?" she said.

"Edmund Hagen," repeated Gemma.

"Oh, my goodness," whispered the lady. "He's the volunteer who sorts the books." She turned around from the counter towards the door at the back of the shop and shouted, "HEY, EDDIE! GET OUT HERE!"

Eddie and Gemma flinched. That lady had a *very* loud voice.

A few moments later, an old man shuffled out from the back of the shop. He wore a brown buttoned-up cardigan. He had a bald head, but huge, wild eyebrows. His wire-rimmed glasses rested on the tip of his nose and looked as if they were about to fall off.

"Yes, yes, I'm coming," he grumbled. "And don't call me Eddie. How many times do I have to tell you? My name is Edmund!"

As Edmund approached the counter, his eyes widened. He put on a little burst of speed and almost leapt forward. "My book!" he cried. "You've found my book!"

"Not me," said the woman. "It was them." She pointed to Eddie and Gemma. "They got the book here last week."

"Oh, my," said Edmund, tears welling up in his eyes. "I thought I had lost it forever." He turned to Eddie and Gemma. "Thank you! Thank you so much."

Eddie smiled. He really hadn't expected to find the book's owner at the op shop. "So you're Edmund Hagen?"

"And you wrote the diary?" added Gemma, astonished.

"In code?" said Eddie.

The two of them started talking over the top of each other.

"Three different codes."

"We managed to decode two of them."

"The Caesar Shift …"

"And the Reverse Letters."

"But we couldn't get the last one."

"You were in an internment camp."

"During World War Two."

"That must have been scary."

"And so unfair."

"And …"

"And …"

"Hold on, hold on," Edmund interrupted them. "You need to slow down and speak one at a time."

"Sorry," said Eddie and Gemma together.

Edmund reached out and carefully picked up his book, turning it over in his hands. "It's not falling apart."

"I fixed it," said Eddie, proudly.

The old man stared at Eddie, wonder in his eyes.

"How about I buy you both a cup of coffee?" he suggested.

"Um … I don't drink coffee," said Eddie.

"Me neither," added Gemma. "Yuck!"

"Hot chocolate, then?" asked Edmund.

The two friends nodded and grinned.

"Sure," said Eddie. "Just let me check with my dad first. He's in the supermarket."

Chapter 9

Hot Chocolate and Codes

"That's an amazing story," said Edmund. "You decoded most of my diary. And you went to all that trouble to find me."

Eddie and Gemma grinned, sipping their hot chocolates.

"And we have the same first name," said Edmund, shaking his head as if he couldn't believe it. "An amazing coincidence, or ..." He paused, raising an eyebrow. "Destiny!" Then a mischievous twinkle sparked in his eyes. "But do you have to shorten it to Eddie? I could cope with Ed, but *Eddie*? It sounds like the sort of name you'd give a toy bear – Teddy Eddie." He snorted into his coffee, sending a little cloud of foam across the table.

Eddie and Gemma laughed.

"How did you lose your book?" asked Gemma.

"I work at the second-hand shop as a volunteer," explained Edmund, "and my job is to sort and price the books. I was taking a break and writing a new message in my diary. A special message for my great-granddaughter. After I finished, I must have got it mixed up with the books that I had sorted, and it ended up on the shelves." He smiled. "I'm lucky that you bought it and not someone else."

The kids grinned again.

"Can you tell us about the diary?" asked Eddie. "And why you wrote it in code? And about that last entry we couldn't work out? Oh, unless it's private."

"Oh … it was just a bit of a game, really," said Edmund. "I was young, you see. Younger than the two of you. World War Two was raging, and I was scared. I was losing all my friends, one by one, because no one wanted to associate with a German during the war."

Edmund looked a little sad.

"I decided I would keep a diary to help fill in the time, but we were very poor and I didn't want to ask my parents for a notebook. I found this damaged book in the rubbish at school. It was unwanted and abandoned, which is how I felt at the time, so I thought I'd use it. And it all became a game."

Edmund gazed off into the distance, remembering. "Never underestimate the positive power of a good game!" He laughed. "I've never lost a game of marbles. And you should see me play hopscotch!"

Then Edmund continued. "There was a book about secret codes in the school library. I liked the idea of the Caesar Shift because I liked history and it connected with the book, seeing as how Shakespeare wrote a play about Julius Caesar. So I used that code. When my family and I were moved to the internment camp, I kept on writing for a little while. I eventually stopped because people were suspicious about what I was doing. So I hid the book and I suppose I forgot about it." He shrugged.

"Years later, when I was a teenager, I came across it," he explained, "and I thought it would be fun to write in it again. It didn't last long, and again, I put it away and forgot about it."

Eddie and Gemma sipped their hot chocolates as Edmund continued his story.

"I rediscovered it earlier this year and I thought I'd give it to my great-granddaughter. She's a smart girl and she likes puzzles, so I thought she would enjoy decoding my writing." He smiled again. "And then I thought I'd write a message to her at the end, in a new code."

He reached into his pocket and pulled out a piece of paper. He unfolded it and placed it on the table. "I made up my own code. I was going to stick this onto the last page of the book so she could decode it."

Eddie and Gemma looked at the paper. It was the key to the last coded entry …

A	B	C	D	E	F	G	H	I	J	K	L	M
8	F	X	W	V	4	T	G	R	Q	I	$	N

N	O	P	Q	R	S	T	U	V	W	X	Y	Z
M	A	K	J	I	D	+	F	E	D	C	B	C

"Talia is a very serious girl," said Edmund. "She spends a lot of time doing schoolwork and helping out her parents at home. I think she needs to have a bit of fun, too. And what better way to have fun than to *play* a game of codes in a book about famous *plays*?" Edmund chuckled. "See what I did there? Wordplay, about playing and plays."

"Talia?" said Gemma, looking surprised. "You don't mean Talia Burke?"

"Yes, that's right," said Edmund. "How did you know?"

"She's in our class at school," said Eddie.

"Wow!" cried Gemma. "Wait until we tell her about all of this."

"Everything is connected," said Edmund with a laugh, his face crinkling and his eyes sparkling. "Just like life."

He pushed the piece of paper with the key across to Eddie and Gemma. Then he slid the book over as well.

"Since you've read the rest of my diary," he said, "would you like to decode the final message?"

Eddie and Gemma nodded eagerly. Eddie whipped out his notebook and pen, and Gemma opened *All the World's a Stage* to the right page. As Gemma read out the letters and numbers and symbols, Eddie used the key and wrote down the decoded words:

You are never too old to play!